SEA-CAT AND
DRAGON KING

SEA-CAT AND DRAGON KING

ANGELA CARTER

Illustrated by
Eva Tatcheva

BLOOMSBURY
CHILDREN'S
BOOKS

First published in Great Britain in 2000
Bloomsbury Publishing Plc, 38 Soho Square, London, W1D 3HB

This paperback edition first published in 2001

The moral right of the author has been asserted
A CIP catalogue record of this book is available from the
British Library

ISBN 0 7475 5267 3

Printed in England by Clays Ltd, St Ives plc

10 9 8 7 6 5 4 3 2 1

To the memory of
Angela Carter – ET

It is a little-known fact that cats live at the bottom of the sea.

Everything at the bottom of the sea is just the same as it is on land – except, of course, that it is quite different.

The creatures who inhabit the countries of the ocean are the same as those who live on dry land but, of course, they are completely different because they are designed to live only in the water.

There are sea-lions, sea-horses, sea-bishops, sea-unicorns, sea-urchins and sea-anemones.

Sea-anemones have very large mouths and are not dumb, like land flowers. Sea-anemones are always chattering away together. They live in clumps and always keep their eyes open, spying for things to gossip about. In fact, they are the greatest gossips you could imagine.

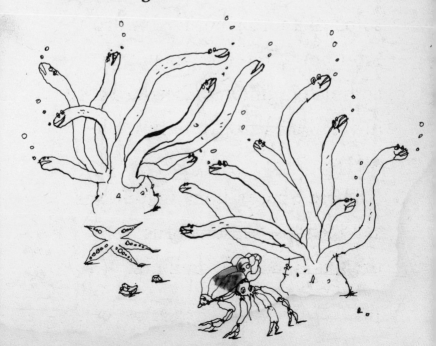

Sea-Cat and his mother lived in
an elegant house with four walls.
The walls were made of pieces of
driftwood of the most fantastic
shapes all woven together, and

though there were many holes,
they did not let the wind through
as there is no wind at the bottom
of the sea.

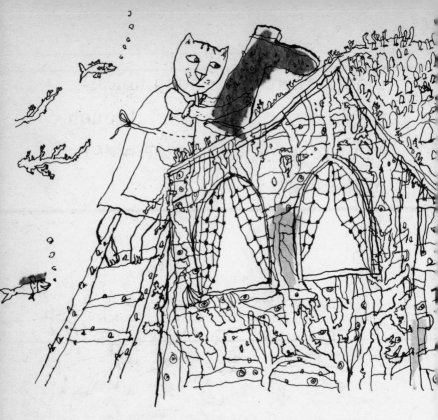

Sea-Cat's mother found an old,
lost sea-boot and set it up at the
corner of the roof for a chimney,
but she never made a fire in that
hearth because fire would never
have burned there, down in the
water. The chimney was only there

to make the house look like a
home. The roof was made of curly
branches of pink and white coral
and the curtains at the windows
were made of fishing nets that
careless fishermen had lost from
their boats.

It was exactly like a land
cottage except that nothing was
the same and no land creature
could possibly have lived in it. But
it had a pleasant garden where
Sea-Cat's mother grew sea-
gooseberries, sea-cucumber and
some bushes of sea-holly, for

Christmas decorations. Every morning, very early, she got up and went out to sternly reprimand the sea-slugs who loved to nibble her vegetables. At night, Sea-Cat

and his mother watched the
starfish twinkle in the night-dark
deep-green water above their
heads until it was time for Sea-Cat
to go to bed.

As, of course, you know, land
cats do not wash well because they
cannot take off their coats of fur.
As soon as a land cat is dipped in
water, his fur coat instantly

becomes matted, soggy, and uncomfortable and it was much the same for Sea-Cat. Sea-Cat's mother worried because Sea-Cat looked like a wet hearthrug and was always catching chills.

But Sea-Cat's mother loved to
knit. Sea-Cat used to go about the
ocean bottom collecting skeins of
seaweed. He held the skeins of
seaweed out between his paws and
his mother wound off ball after

ball of seaweed knitting wool.
Sea-Cat's mother also loved to
embroider. She went out by
herself, picked up all manner of
forsaken treasures from the ocean
bottom and carried them home in
her apron.

She collected every kind of shell; from wrecks of ships she collected pieces of tin plate that were just like silver sequins; she collected little bits of bottle glass, smoothed and polished by the sea until they were just like jewels. Then she sat down in her rocking chair and knitted and embroidered everything into a closely fitting, elegantly tailored, wonderfully complicated, waterproof, decorative, scintillating catsuit for Sea-Cat to wear. So, although Sea-Cat lived deep beneath the waves, he was always snug and cosy, and, besides, he shone most beautifully. Sea-Cat shone like a wet star.

Sea-Cat was dressed in all the
colours of the rainbow which
arches constantly over the realms
under the sea whenever the sun

shines through the water, because under the sea, it is just as if it were always raining. But everybody is used to it so nobody complains about the weather.

Even when he went to bed, Sea-
Cat did not take off his
waterproof suit because it was so
beautiful and he was so

comfortable when he wore it. In
fact, he only ever took off his suit
in order to have a bath. In the
ocean, the sea creatures wash

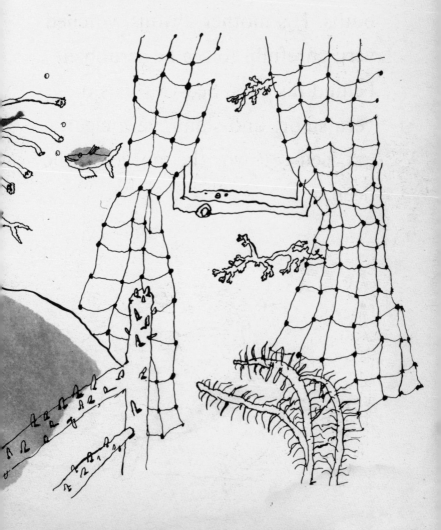

themselves by rubbing themselves
very thoroughly, all over, with the
driest sand they can find. So that
was the way that Sea-Cat took his
baths. His mother always watched
very carefully to see he scrubbed
behind his ears. Sea-Cat was a
very smart and shiny, very clean
cat. Sea-Cat was the marvel of the
deep.

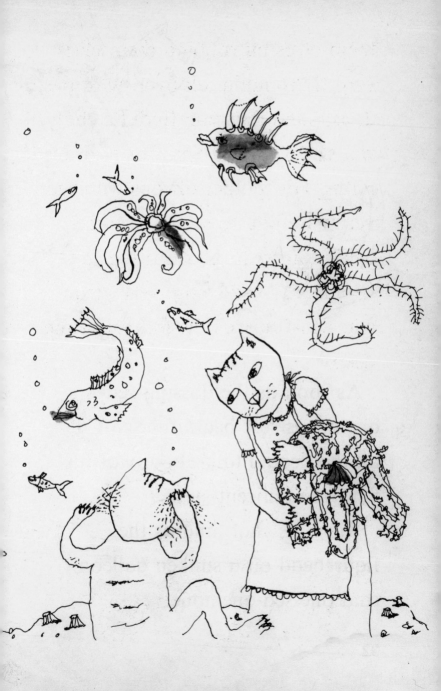

As soon as the gossipy sea-
anemones saw beautiful Sea-Cat,
all they could talk about was his
new, magnificent suit.

'He is as charming as the
figurehead on a sunken galleon!'
said one sea-anemone.

'He is lovelier than an oyster full of pearls!' said another sea-anemone.

'He is more delightful than the sunshine shining through the water!' said a third sea-anemone.

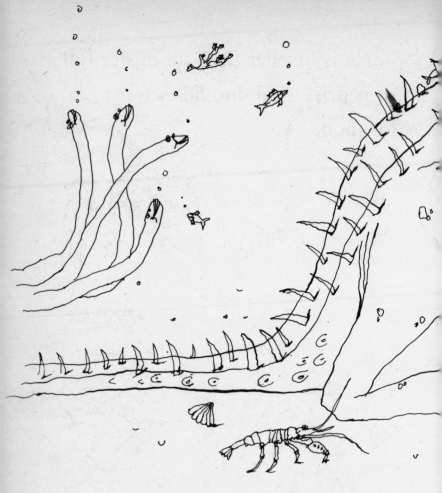

Dragon King overheard them.
Dragon King was Lord of the
Ocean. Nobody knew how old
Dragon King was. Some people

said he was as old as time itself
and others said he was a little
older. And he was as ugly as he
was old. He was the shape, more

or less, of a peculiar fish or whale but he was of an excessive and clumsy size and he did not have smoothly interlocking scales to cover himself. Instead, he had a hide covered with knobs, warts, lumps, bumps, carbuncles and wrinkles. He was as wise and kind as a Dragon King could be, but his eyes were always sad because he was ashamed of his ugliness.

He was so ashamed of his ugliness he liked to go about his dominions in absolute secrecy. He lurked furtively behind boulders and crept uneasily along the sea bottom, where he was almost invisible because he was exactly the colour of mud. And although he was Lord of the Ocean, nobody admired him because he did not admire himself.

He always used to be a great
eavesdropper because he hoped
that, one fine day, he would
overhear somebody say:
'Goodness. How beautiful Dragon
King is!'

Dragon King knew that he was
the ugliest creature who ever lived.
In all of his extraordinarily long
life he had never seen anyone half
as ugly as he was. He had only
ever dared look in a looking-glass

once in his life; once was enough.
But still he hoped against hope
that the looking-glass had lied to
him. He hoped that in reality he
was as beautiful as a star and that
one day he would overhear
somebody say so.

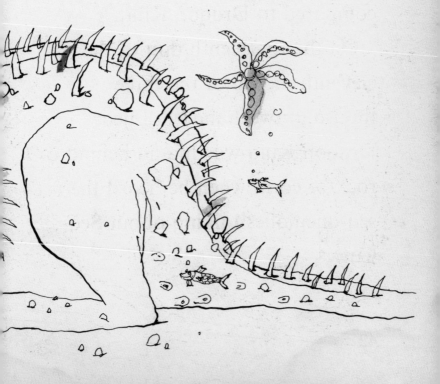

For three thousand two hundred years, eleven months and thirteen days, Dragon King crept about the ocean listening in to all the whispering and yet he never heard even the littlest sea-slug say: 'My, but Dragon King is beautiful!'

For even a sea-slug is beautiful compared to Dragon King.

On the fourteenth day of the eleventh month of the three thousand two hundredth year, Dragon King was hiding behind a rock of coral when he heard the sea-anemones talking about Sea-Cat.

'When Sea-Cat wears the suit his mother made him, he shines like a wet star! Sea-Cat is the marvel of the deep!'

Dragon King forgot his
centuries of wisdom and became
so jealous he immediately turned
the brightest of all possible greens.
His fins quivered and he thrashed
his tail so much that he disturbed

the entire sea bottom and vanished
altogether inside a cloud of
swirling mud.

'When he takes off his suit,
Sea-Cat is nothing but a wet
hearthrug,' he said to himself. 'But
when he is dressed up, everyone

admires him. If I could put on his suit, I would be just as beautiful as Sea-Cat and then I would have enough self-confidence to walk proudly about the ocean, just as a Dragon King should!'

Sea-Cat was out gathering seaweed for his mother so that she could knit mufflers for the sea-lions, who often suffered from sore throats due to too much roaring. (When a sea-lion has a sore throat, he likes to comfort it with a muffler.)

Dragon King took a big sack with him. He crept up behind Sea-Cat and dropped the sack over Sea-Cat's head. He scooped up Sea-Cat in a protesting bundle and swam triumphantly away to his enormous, miserable palace.

Dragon King's palace was made out of the skeleton of a whale, so it was like a very big cage made of ivory and Dragon King sat in it all by himself because he did not wish to expose his ugliness to any

servants. His palace was furnished
with gilded thrones salvaged from
the wrecks of Spanish galleons,
silver candlesticks salvaged from
the wrecks of tea clippers, and all
manner of other treasures. It had

a regal atmosphere but the emptiness and silence made it the saddest of all places in which to live. Though there were no mirrors, many flattering pictures of Dragon King hung on the ribs of the whale which were the walls. Dragon King painted these portraits himself, in his spare time, out of a wistful desire to see himself as somebody beautiful.

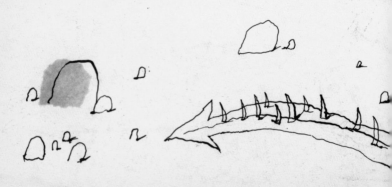

As soon as they reached this
unhomelike home, Dragon King
emptied Sea-Cat out of his sack.
Sea-Cat was the most beautiful
thing that ever was seen in this
gloomy palace.

'Now I have you in my power,
Sea-Cat. Give me your beautiful
suit and I will let you go.'

Sea-Cat glittered like flowers in the rain.

'Why do you want my beautiful suit?'

'If I wear your beautiful suit, I will become as beautiful as you.'

'But,' said Sea-Cat, who was practical, like all cats, 'if I give you my suit, my fur will instantly get all matted, soggy and uncomfortable.'

'If you give me your beautiful suit, I will make you a Duke of the Deep Sea. Then you will feel far too important ever to be uncomfortable.'

But Sea-Cat looked at Dragon King and saw what a strange shape he was.

'Anyway,' said Sea-Cat, 'even if I give you my beautiful suit, it will never fit you because you are a different size to me.'

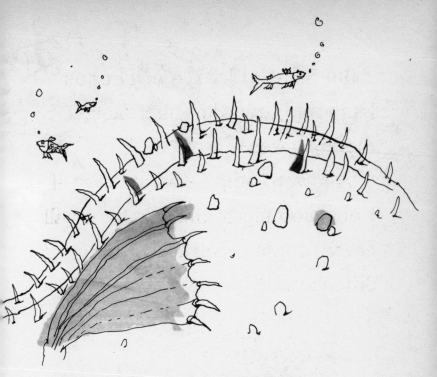

Sea-Cat was far too polite to say that Dragon King was not only a different size but also covered in all manner of lumps and bumps which would burst through the fabric of his elegantly tailored catsuit at innumerable places.

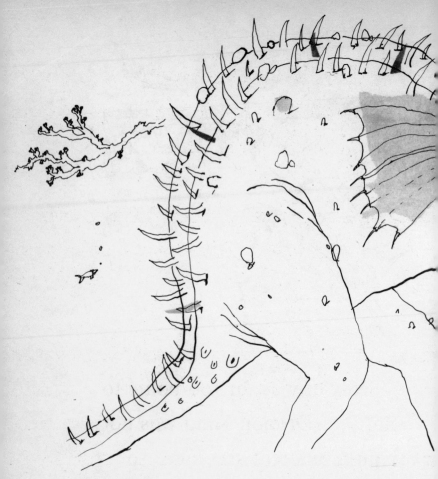

Dragon King wanted Sea-Cat's
suit so much he lost his patience
and tried to exercise his authority.
He became pompous and
arrogant.

'Give me your beautiful suit
because I am Dragon King, Lord
of the Ocean, and I am much
more important than a humble
little Sea-Cat.'

But Sea-Cat knew he was important because his mother loved him and he said: 'I can never give away my catsuit because my mother knitted it for me and I could never give away my mother's present, because she knitted it for me with love.'

Dragon King thought to
himself: 'Nobody will ever give me
a present because they love me!'
He forgot that he wanted the suit
only in order to make him

beautiful; he remembered only
that he had nobody to knit him
even so much as a nightcap, to
keep his head warm in winter, in
his lonely bed. Then Dragon King
began to cry.

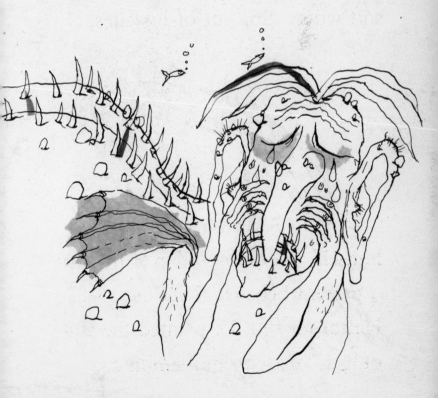

Now, as everybody who lives in
the ocean knows, Dragon King
cries tears of rubies, for if he
cried tears of salty water nobody
would know that he was crying
because everywhere, there, is
salt water. So, out of his eyes,

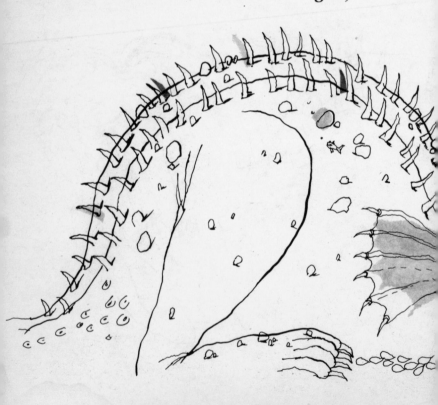

came plopping hundreds of
rubies, for he was crying very
bitterly. And the more he cried,
the more rubies there were, until
Dragon King and Sea-Cat were
standing in a great heap of
rubies.

'Oh!' wailed Dragon King. 'I do so want to be beautiful! Although I am Lord of the Ocean, nobody loves me because I am so ugly!'

Sea-Cat felt sorry for Dragon King, all alone and lonely in his

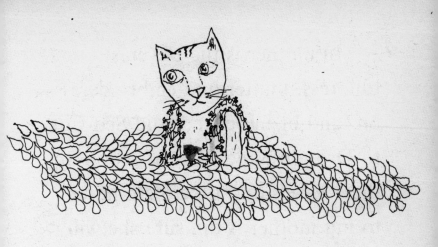

sad palace, with all the flattering
pictures of himself on the walls
that did not comfort him. But the
pile of rubies grew bigger and
bigger, and glittered more and
more brightly, until they shone
more brightly even than Sea-Cat's
suit and Sea-Cat and Dragon
King stood up to their shoulders
in rubies. At that, Sea-Cat had an
idea.

'My mother is the cleverest tailoress, knitter and embroideress on land or in ocean,' said Sea-Cat to Dragon King. 'Let us scoop up these jewels and take them home to my mother. I am sure she will think of some way to dress you up handsomely and the jewels will come in handy to embroider your suit.'

'Are you sure that your mother will like me?' asked Dragon King doubtfully. 'After all, I am very, very ugly.'

Sea-Cat was deeply touched.

'Oh no!' he cried. 'She will be honoured to meet you because you

are Dragon King. And she will
admire your colour because it is
such a practical brown.'

So they put all the rubies in the
sack with which Dragon King had
trapped Sea-Cat and went home
together to Sea-Cat's mother's
cottage.

Night was falling.

Sea-Cat's mother stood at the
gate, wondering whatever had
become of Sea-Cat. Indoors, on

the driftwood table, a salad of
sea-cucumbers was sliced ready
and waiting for supper.

She was astonished to see Sea-Cat coming home with Dragon King. She had heard of Dragon King, of course, but she had never seen him and, because she had a very kind heart, she was sorry for him because he was so ugly and self-conscious.

Sea-Cat and Dragon King
carried a huge bulging sack
between them but the sack was not
heavy to carry because the water
through which they moved buoyed
it up. Sea-Cat glistened like a
Christmas tree but Dragon King
was as drab as a fish made all of
mud.

'Mother, Mother, could you knit
a beautiful suit such as mine for
our distinguished guest?' asked
Sea-Cat.

'I will measure him up as soon
as we have had supper,' said Sea-
Cat's mother.

So they ate a good supper, first.
Then Sea-Cat's mother measured
Dragon King with her tape
measure. He was of immense size,
and not one square inch of him
was smooth in texture, but she
walked all round him and made a
number of complicated diagrams.

Then she emptied out the rubies
and gasped at their magnificence.

'I will make a suit truly fit for a
Dragon King!' she promised.

The next morning, bright and
early, after a refreshing night's

sleep, she sent Sea-Cat and
Dragon King out to gather
enough seaweed for a very big,
very splendid Dragon King suit.
Then they both helped her wind
off a hundred balls of sea-wool.

Dragon King found it was very pleasant to sit and chat with his new friends as they wound off the wool together; it was far more pleasant than sitting alone in his enormous palace, wishing he were beautiful.

So Dragon King, Lord of the
Ocean, lived in Sea-Cat's mother's
cottage and helped her with the
washing up while she knitted,
knitted, knitted away for seven
whole days and seven whole
nights. Then it took her another
seven whole days and seven whole
nights to embroider the waterproof
suit all over with rubies.

When the suit was finished, it
glowed like flowers in sunshine. It
glowed like port wine in the glass.
It glowed like the rose window in
a cathedral.

'Oh!' said Dragon King. The
suit will make me more beautiful
than anything else in the entire
ocean!'

'No,' said Sea-Cat's mother. The suit will only make you look beautiful.'

'Well,' said Dragon King. 'That is very much better than nothing.'

So he tried it on and then he looked at himself in Sea-Cat's mother's long mirror. He had not looked at himself for more than three thousand years.

If Sea-Cat shone like a wet star,
Dragon King shone like the sun
beneath the ocean.

He was as red as a sunset.

He looked as magnificent as a
Dragon King should look.

He was a complete festival in
himself alone.

'I am far more imposing than even the most imposing of my self-portraits,' he said. 'Now I can walk out and about just as the Lord of the Ocean should.'

'However, the suit is only a covering,' said Sea-Cat's mother. 'Now you no longer feel shy, you must continue to be wise.'

'Yes,' said Dragon King. 'It is not my suit but your suit. I owe all my new magnificence to Sea-Cat's mother and Sea-Cat, who invited me to his home.'

So he instantly made Sea-Cat's mother a sea-duchess and Sea-Cat a sea-duke, and they went out

together into the underwater
world.

All the creatures of the ocean
bottom came swimming up to see

them and clapped their finny
hands together in applause. While

the noisy sea-anemones cried;

'Hurrah! Hurrah! Hurrah! There is nothing in the sea or out of it half as splendid as Sea-Cat and Dragon King and nobody anywhere even so much as a quarter as clever as Sea-Cat's mother!'

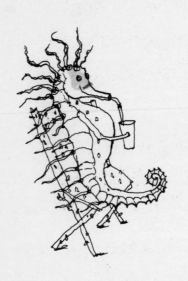